Don't Dilly Dally,

Silly Sally

Don't Dilly Dally, Silly Sally

By Marc Ferrari

Illustration by Felipe Diaz Huarnez

BELLE ISLE BOOKS
www.belleislebooks.com

ISBN: 978-1-9399308-1-1

Library of Congress Control Number: 2016949827

Printed in the United States

Published by

BELLE ISLE BOOKS
www.belleislebooks.com

This book is dedicated to all the Silly Sallys of the world
who march to the time of their own beat,
and to the parents, grandparents, and caregivers
who love them for it.

Sally was a silly girl,
as silly as can be.
She loved to play her silly games.
She always was carefree.

Sally was so very smart,
and equally delightful.
It's just that when it came to time,
she wasn't quite so mindful!

Sally liked to take her time.
It always made her late.
Sometimes her parents would get mad,
and that was not so great.

Don't dilly dally, Silly Sally!
We've got things to do!
People to see, places to go,
and we're always waiting on you!

Every morning she had school,
Sally would be so slow.
Her father tried to nudge her,
"Come on, it's time to go!"

Whenever she had homework
or chores she had begun,
Sally would procrastinate,
and nothing would get done!

And when she had to be somewhere,
most times she barely made it.
'Cause if they tried to leave on time,
Sally always delayed it.

Don't dilly dally, Silly Sally!
Let's try to get a move on!
We've got lots of plans today.
It's time to get your groove on!

THEN ONE DAY...

Sally got invited to
her best friend's birthday party.
A special boat ride on the lake!
No way could she be tardy.

As Sally counted down the days,
she grew most excited.
She could hardly wait to see her friends.
Everyone would be delighted!

But when that special day arrived,
Sally did not mind the clock,
and by the time they made it there,
the boat had left the dock!

Don't dilly dally, Silly Sally!
'Cause things will start without you.
Your friends will wonder where you are—
They'll be talking all about you!

On the boat, the children wondered
Where could Sally be?
Did their car run out of gas?
Was she stuck up in a tree?

Sally was so very sad
and so were all her friends.
She said, "I know it's all my fault,
I'll try to make amends.

I learned my lesson and now I know
sometimes I cannot dawdle.
'Cause if I miss more special things,
I will feel just awful!"

"I'll do my best to not be late,
so we don't have to hurry.
I'll give myself some <u>EXTRA</u> time,
so we won't have to worry!

If I just give a real good try,
I know that I can do it!
I can do a better job,
and now I'm gonna prove it!"

SO NOW...

Sally doesn't dilly dally
as much as she did before.
In fact, she has become quite prompt.
She's the *first* one out the door!

ACKNOWLEDGEMENTS

The author wishes to thank

Peter Thall

Tom Sturges

the entire staff of Brandylane Publishers / Belle Isle Books

my parents

my beautiful wife Lorraine

and my amazingly awesome daughter Sierra,

who was the inspiration for this book.

About the Author

Marc Ferrari is a former major label recording artist, music publishing executive, film and TV actor, and published author. He has sold over 2 million albums, toured the world alongside some of music's most popular bands, appeared in the hit movies *Wayne's World* and *Wayne's World 2*, and has written music that has been used in over 500 network TV shows and major motion pictures. But screaming fans, fawning minions, and all the trappings of fame could not prepare Ferrari for his biggest challenge: settling down to a life of domesticity and becoming father to a precocious, oblivious-to-time daughter who tests him in ways he never imagined! Ferrari lives in Los Angeles with his wife, daughter, and a slew of family pets.

About the Illustrator

Felipe Diaz Huarnez is a professional illustrator and comic artist from Santiago, Chile. He holds a degree in illustration from the professional Institute of Arts and Communication (ARCOS) and works as an international freelancer specializing in children's book illustration and comic art. He has illustrated several children's books, including *The New Wheelchair, Lady on the Run,* and *El Clavileño Dos,* and illustrated the cover/back cover art for *Al Infinito: Cuentos de Carreteras.*